THE FANTASTIC FLATULENT
FART BROTHERS

GO TO THE
MOON!

M.D. Whalen

illustrated by Des Campbell

Publisher's Cataloging-in-Publication Data

Names: Whalen, M.D., author. | Campbell, Des., illustrator.
Title: The fantastic flatulent fart brothers go to the moon! A spaced out
  adventure that truly stinks / M.D Whalen; illustrated by Des Campbell.
Series: The Fantastic Flatulent Fart Brothers
Description: Silvermine Bay, Hong Kong: Top Floor Books, 2017.
Summary: After stowing away on a lunar mission, brothers Willy and
  Peter and their sister's hamster save the moon from flatulent aliens
  from Uranus.
Identifiers: ISBN 9789627866312 (pbk., USA) | 9789627866329 (pbk., UK) |
  9789627866336 (ebook, USA) | 9789627866343 (ebook, UK)
Subjects: LCSH Space flight–Juvenile fiction. | Moon–Juvenile fiction.
  | Human-alien encounters–Juvenile fiction. | Flatulence–Juvenile
  fiction. | Brothers–Juvenile fiction. | Humorous stories. | Science
  fiction. | CYAC Space flight–Fiction. | Moon–Fiction. | Human-alien
  encounters–Fiction. | Flatulence–Fiction. | Brothers–Fiction. | BISAC
  JUVENILE FICTION / Humorous Stories | JUVENILE FICTION / Science
  Fiction | JUVENILE FICTION / Action & Adventure / General
Classification: LCC PZ7.1 .W4378 Fa 2017 | DDC [Fic]–dc23

ISBN 978 962 7866 31 2
First US edition, published 2017

Top Floor Books
PO Box 29
Silvermine Bay, Hong Kong
topfloorbooks.com

CONTENTS

CHAPTER 1
Second Sheep

Willy wished he had someone to play games with besides his big brother Peter.

Right now Peter was picking a thick brown scab off his leg, when he should have been concentrating on the giant saber-toothed worm monsters battling the Trans-Galactic Imperial Infantry.

"Gross!" Willy dropped his game controller in disgust. "You let one get away!"

"Oh yeah? This'll stop him." Peter lifted one butt cheek and let out a blustery paint peeler of a fart.

That called for revenge. Willy raised his rear end and spewed a dirty green booty blast so rotten-smelling it could have melted steel, or one of the Dorlusian robot gladiators that had just stomped into view.

"Now *you're* the one who lost us points!" Peter said. "Just for that, eat this." He tore another scab from his knee and spun it at him. Willy ducked just in time.

"Uh oh," Peter said, his nose pointing behind Willy.

The scab stuck to the forehead of their little sister Skyler, who didn't seem to notice as she skipped happily down the stairs. She hopped in front of the couch and held out two slips of paper.

"For my special brothers," Skyler said.

"We don't need toilet paper," Peter said, winking at Willy.

"This isn't toilet paper, dummy," Skyler said. "These are VIP tickets for my kindergarten spring pageant. We're performing 'Old MacDonald Had a Farm.'"

"And what are you, one of the pigs?" Peter imitated a snorting hog.

Skyler ignored him and stuck up her nose. "I play Lamb Number Two, the second-most important sheep in the whole play."

"Hey, know what a sheep fart sounds like?" Peter squeezed out a honk that sounded more goosey than sheepy.

"Don't be disgusting. You better come!" Skyler set the tickets between them on the couch. "Oh yeah, one more thing. I need you to babysit Squeaky."

Squeaky was Skyler's pet hamster. All he did all day was crack sunflower seeds and run inside his wheel.

Once he'd bitten Willy's finger, one of the most painful experiences in his life. Though to his credit, Squeaky often lived up to his name with hilarious little hamster farts.

"We actors are required at rehearsal," Skyler said. She placed a grapefruit-sized clear plastic hamster ball on the floor. "So please look after–"

KABOOM!

A terrifying explosion cut her off.

"See what you made happen?" Peter tossed his controller on the floor. "You let the Trans-Galactic Star Station blow up!"

Big red words appeared on the screen: "You lost the battle. Go back to Level 12."

Before either boy could punish their sister with a lethal fart, she was out the door. With Peter's scab still stuck to her head, at least.

"Who wants to sit through some stupid kidney-garden pageant to watch her bleat like a sheep?" Peter said.

Willy agreed. "We need to get away, as far away as possible."

Peter switched the television to a regular station, but it was just the news. He was about to press another channel, when Willy said, "Hold it!"

WIND-BREAKING NEWS

Moon mission lift-off today — Moon

The news showed a rocket on a launchpad, while the reporter reported: "...first manned mission to the Moon in forty years. The public is invited to meet the astronauts today, just before lift-off, at the Gasserton Space Command Center auditorium."

"Cool! That's in the next town," Willy said.

Peter was already out of his seat. "Let's go!"

They packed snacks for the ride over: nacho corn chips, refried beans, hard boiled eggs, plus a bag of leftover onion rings. Then they ran down the street to catch the bus.

"Wait!" Willy said. "We promised to babysit the hamster."

"I don't remember any promise," Peter said.

Willy looked away, so his brother wouldn't see his tear-filled eyes. They couldn't leave poor little Squeaky all alone in the house. What if a pet thief broke in?

Willy dashed home, scooped up the hamster ball, and reached the bus stop just in time.

"Do you see what I see?" Peter said.

Willy saw. The bus was jam-packed with student ballerinas.

They settled in the back seat. "Pass the eggs and beans and onion rings," Peter said.

Ten blocks later they hammered out nose-melting, eye-watering fart bombs that turned the air in the bus grungy yellow.

One block after that, their butts hit the sidewalk.

The next bus came along after a few minutes. This one was filled with an old ladies' knitting club.

Willy and Peter gulped down another can of beans. This was turning out to be a truly fun day.

CHAPTER 2
The Evil Doorman

A crooked-nosed doorman stopped them at the Space Command Center entrance.

"Got tickets?"

"No one told us we needed tickets," Willy said.

"Tough luck. All sold out," the doorman said.

Willy was about to cry, but Peter winked at him and told the guard, "Sure we got tickets."

Peter pulled out the paper that Skyler had given him earlier, and Willy did the same. They started to walk past, until monstrous hands gripped their shoulders.

"Says right here these are for Old MacDonald," the doorman said. "Not old Man in the Moon. Anyway, no pets."

He pointed to a sign which read:

No Animals Allowed, Including
Snakes, Spiders, and Hamsters

"Now, scram!" The doorman balled up the tickets and tossed them aside.

Peter led Willy around the corner, where they hid behind a tree. "Time to use our foolproof method for getting past guards. Start eating."

Peter opened the bag of cold, greasy onion rings and poured bean dip all over them. For good measure, he shoved hard-boiled eggs in his and Willy's mouths.

A few minutes later, they were back in front of the doorman.

"Hey, I thought I told you guys—"

Willy and Peter dropped their pants and pumped out loud, bubbly brown fart blasts that smelled like a garbage dump had exploded. Some late arrivals ran away, but the doorman just stood there.

"That's nothing," he told them. "Just had my lunch at a taco truck." He bent over, aiming his rear end like a cannon.

A fart struck Willy in the face like a boxing glove, sending him somersaulting backwards down the steps.

"Aaaaaaahhhhh!" Willy screamed.

"Ooooooogggg!" Peter followed, gagging and retching.

The doorman laughed like an evil troll. "Har har har! Don't let me catch you brats showing your faces—or butts—around here again."

Willy wanted to cry. His chance of a lifetime, to meet real, live astronauts! Ruined! Peter patted Willy's shoulder and said not to worry, they would find a way in.

They snuck around the side of the building and tried a few doors. At one, another guard yelled at them. The rest of the doors were locked.

Finally they came to a door where they heard voices inside.

Peter had an idea. He put Squeaky in his hamster ball right next to the door. He knocked, then they both ran and hid behind a bush.

The door opened a crack. A man's head peered out, looked right and left, shrugged, then went back inside and let the door close behind him. Except it didn't shut completely—it was stuck against the hamster ball.

Willy and Peter tiptoed over and listened until the voices and footsteps faded.

They were in!

CHAPTER 3

Rocket Man

Willy and Peter crept through an empty white hallway, past unmarked white doors. Hearing more voices ahead, they ducked into the nearest room.

It looked like the changing room at the school gym, only without the sweaty smell. Peter pointed to the tall lockers lining one wall.

"Let's hide in there!" He swung open a locker door.

"Whoa!" Peter and Willy said at the same time.

They were staring at a big, white astronaut space suit!

The next locker contained another.

"Let's try them on!" Peter said, dragging out the first space suit.

Willy thought this was a great idea and a bad idea at the same time. They were in deep trouble just by being here. But who could resist the fun?

The second space suit was stiff and a bit heavy, and way too big for him, but once he clipped on the helmet he felt like a real astronaut.

This was awesome! They waved their arms like space aliens and made silly faces at each other.

Peter's mouth puckered, his eyebrows jammed together. Willy knew what was coming.

Peter's fart reverberated through his suit and echoed off the walls. Of course, Willy had to fart in response. Then he wished he hadn't eaten those hard-boiled eggs.

Willy struggled to breathe inside the sealed space suit. Where was the oxygen tank on this thing?

Suddenly the voices in the hallway grew louder. They climbed out of the suits as quickly as they could, then clamped the helmets back on, so no tell-tale smell would escape, and shoved the suits back in the lockers. There was a toilet stall in the corner. With nowhere else to hide, they shut themselves inside.

"The hamster ball!" Peter whispered.

Willy rushed out, grabbed Squeaky and returned just in time. The outside door opened and he heard two men speaking. They were the astronauts!

"Commander, how many minutes they keeping us on stage?" one said.

"Think about ten," the other said. "Got a full house. Though I hear a class of ballerinas and a ladies' knitting club canceled due to sudden illness. So it's mostly primary school brats."

"Yeah, gonna be the same old dumb questions. 'What happens if you fart in your space suit?'"

"'What happens if you need to barf in space?'"

"'What if you have to scratch your butt during a space walk?'"

Inside the toilet stall, Willy nodded. Those were the exact questions he'd been planning to ask. He heard the clack of the lockers opening. The space suits being taken out. Some muttering about a faint smell. Heard the astronauts climbing into their suits and the snap of the helmets being fastened.

This was followed by muffled coughing inside the space suits, which turned into gasping and gagging.

Willy turned to Peter, who looked just as frightened as he himself felt. They peeked under the toilet stall door.

Both astronauts staggered around the room, gurgling and retching, desperately trying to undo the fasteners on their helmets. One tripped over a changing bench, fell flat on his back, and lay still.

The other spun in circles, yanking open one of his helmet clasps, but it was too late.

His knees folded, his body twisted, eyes rolled up in his head. He crumpled against the toilet stall door.

"We're in humongous trouble," Willy said. "They're going to come looking for them."

"Maybe not. Give me a hand," Peter said.

They opened the stall door and dragged the nearest astronaut inside. He was stone cold unconscious. They propped him up into sitting position on the toilet seat, then latched the door shut and crawled out underneath.

The other astronaut lay sprawled across the floor. Peter made sure he was still zonked out, then they removed his helmet and pulled the astronaut out of the space suit.

"Eww," Willy said. The astronaut wore nothing but stretchy long underwear.

Squeaky came over and checked out the helmet, as if it was another hamster ball. It was so cute, Willy took out his phone to snap a picture, but just then new footsteps sounded in the hallway.

They shoved the half-naked astronaut in the locker.

"Only one way out of here," Peter said, nodding at the space suit. "You get in first, and I'll stand on your shoulders."

"No way!" Willy said. "You're heavier than me."

"Yeah, but I look older."

"Stupider, too."

"Be quiet. Tell you what, we'll take turns. You go first on the bottom, and later we switch places."

Willy's eyes teared up at the stink inside the suit, like a family of skunks had died in there, which Willy of course recognized as his own stink. That was at least better than breathing in his brother's stale farts. Peter handed down the hamster ball and the bag with the rest of their snacks.

The footsteps paused at the door.

Peter crawled into the space suit and pulled on the helmet just as the door flew open.

"Show time, gentlemen," said a man's voice. "Phew. What's that smell?"

CHAPTER 4
Space Puke

"**H**ow you doing, Commander?" the man said, not realizing that Peter and Willy were inside the space suit.

"Hey, no wonder it stinks in here."

Willy couldn't see, but he heard the man knock on the toilet stall door.

"Lieutenant Samson, finish your business quick, then suit up and come to the auditorium. I'll escort Commander Major to the stage to get started."

He slapped the back of the space suit.

"Let's get out of here, Commander. Lucky you've got a helmet on. Yuck! What a stench!"

Between Peter's weight on his shoulders, and the fact that his feet didn't reach the end of the space boots, Willy had a tough time walking. He slid one leg forward, then the other, while Peter whispered, "Turn right here, turn left there." Meanwhile, Squeaky rolled his ball in circles around Willy's neck.

Willy wished they'd never gotten into this predicament. He wished he'd never listened to his brother. *Ew!* Did Peter just blast a silent stinker in his face? Right now he wished he'd never been born.

Soon he heard clapping and cheering. They were on the stage.

"We're dead men," Willy said.

"Shh! Just two more steps. Yeah. Now turn left. Okay, stop."

Peter waved to the crowd. The cheering grew louder. Then a woman introduced Astronaut Tom Major, Commander of the first manned Moon mission of this century.

"Commander, are you able to take a bow in that suit?"

"Please, no," Willy said.

"Come on, we've got to kill ten minutes," Peter whispered.

Peter leaned forward and promptly lost his balance. Willy grabbed Peter's legs, but it was too late. The space helmet smacked against the podium.

Squeaky rolled around Willy's face, chattering so loud it was picked up by the microphone and broadcast through the auditorium speakers. The audience laughed while Peter straightened up.

The woman announcer said, "Why don't we open up for questions. The boy in the fourth row with the green shirt."

"Um, Captain? What happens when you have to fart in space?"

Peter put on his deepest adult voice impersonation. "You mean like this?"

"Don't you dare," Willy said.

Peter dared. He honked out a blast that sounded like a brass band and smelled like rotten dinosaur eggs.

The audience roared hysterically, which was lucky, since nobody could hear Willy's gagging.

"That does it!" Willy hissed between coughs. "Time to switch places."

"Aw, it was just starting to get fun."

Peter and Willy scrambled and clawed their way over each other. It must have looked really weird, like the "astronaut" was having convulsions, because some girls screamed.

"Commander! Are you all right?" the woman announcer said.

"Sure," Willy said in his deepest voice, which wasn't deep at all. "Um. Got a wedgie in my undies. Hard to shake loose in a space suit."

Willy got his first look at the auditorium. Almost every seat was filled with kids. He recognized some from his school. If only they knew!

He guessed they probably had another seven minutes left. What if someone asked a science question or something? He had to fill the time to avoid that. He also wanted revenge.

"But getting back to farts," he said, "sometimes astronauts fart like this."

Peter's protest was drowned by Willy's grand performance: leading with a high squealer, down to a splattering lawn mower engine, then ending with a deep, watery butt gargle. Peter swooned beneath him. Served him right.

The audience went mad. Adults screamed. Kids fell off their seats. Hundreds of people let off their own farts.

Willy eyed the wall clock: five and a half minutes to go.

"Enough on that topic," the woman speaker said. "Another question?"

A hundred hands shot in the air. Willy was about to point to a girl, then realized she lived just down the street, and might recognize his voice.

He pointed to another girl with frizzy hair in a middle row.

"Excuse me for asking this, sir, but... I mean...what happens when you barf in space?"

"You mean like this?" Willy said.

Peter pinched Willy's leg really hard, and whispered, "I'll kill you."

"Just kidding!" said Willy. Everyone laughed.

The woman speaker pointed to a boy in a side seat.

"What happens if you're out on a space

walk and your butt itches? How do you scratch it?"

Four minutes to go. Willy couldn't think of an answer.

Just then he felt Squeaky rolling around his feet. "Hamsters. We keep hamsters inside our space suits, so when we itch, they can go there and scratch us with their claws."

People nodded as if this made sense. A few kids raise their phones to take photos.

Just in time Willy put his hand in front of the visor. What if people enlarged the pictures and recognized his face?

"No photos, please, children. You might blind the astronauts," said the woman.

"Speaking of which, I've just been told that lift-off to the Moon is in fifteen minutes! Let's thank Commander Tom

Major with a big round of applause."

A man tugged Willy's arm and said, "Let's go, Commander. You've got a rocket to catch."

Willy thought, *What have we gotten ourselves into?*

CHAPTER 5

The EMU Lab

A skinny guy with thick black-rimmed glasses introduced himself as Mister Chan. He led them through a long white hallway that seemed to go on forever.

Peter moaned and groaned about all the walking.

"No fair," he whispered. "Time to switch places again."

"What'd you say, Commander?" Chan said.

Willy belched his words, hoping it

sounded deeper than his little kid voice.

"Urp! You go ahead, Mister Chan. I need to tie my shoes."

"Space suits don't have shoelaces," Peter whispered.

"Be quiet," Willy said.

"Huh? I didn't say anything," Chan said. "But okay, I've got to get to my station. You know the way: end of the hall, turn right, take the elevator."

They waited for Chan to leave, then Willy told Peter, "Turn left."

They slipped through a door into a dark room.

"What are we going to do?" Willy panted.

They both climbed out of the space suit, then Peter switched on the light.

"Whoa!" Willy and Peter said at the same time.

A sign on the wall said:

EXTRAVEHICULAR MOBILITY UNIT (EMU) EXPERIMENTAL LAB

EMU must be what they called space suits. The room was full of them.

Some were super-tall; others had big round mid-sections, maybe for pregnant lady astronauts. Some looked like they were straight out of futuristic comic books.

"I don't believe this," Peter said. "Look!"

He pointed to a space suit—that is, EMU—with four skinny legs.

"This must be for space dogs," Peter said. "Can you imagine chasing a ball in zero gravity?"

"Or spraying an interstellar fire hydrant," Willy said.

But the greatest thing they found was in a side closet: half a dozen kid-sized suits.

Willy tried on the smallest one. It was a still a little big, but he could see fine

through the helmet.

"Hey, this one fits me perfect," Peter said, examining the buttons and controls on his suit.

"Wait a second," Willy said. "We need

41

to talk."

Willy shivered, maybe from fear, or maybe because the room was ice cold. He wiped his runny nose, then licked the snot from his space glove.

"If we go out there, we're in huge trouble. First, we knocked out two astronauts. We could go to jail for that."

Peter nodded. "True."

"And these space suits. We could get life sentences for stealing government property."

"Uh huh."

"And if we actually go into space, that's driving a spaceship without a license. Add hard labor. Or worse."

Peter nodded again. "Could be."

"Or we might lose control of the ship and get lost in space, drifting through empty blackness until we starve to death or run out of oxygen. Or get smashed into by an asteroid and explode."

Peter nodded once more.

"And if we stay on Earth, then we have to watch our sister play a sheep."

"Eeuw," Willy said, strapping on his helmet.

"Moon, here we come!"

CHAPTER 6

Having A Blast

The hallway was empty; the coast was clear. Willy grabbed the hamster. Peter took their bag of snacks.

They ran down the corridor as fast as they could—which wasn't very fast in full space suits—then around the corner, into the elevator, and pressed the button for the top platform.

When they got out, people were too busy checking computers to notice two very short astronauts dashing across the platform into the waiting space capsule.

Peter tripped on the way in. Corn chips scattered everywhere.

"Quick! Close the hatch!" Willy said.

It took both of them to push the heavy door closed and lock the handle. Safe at last! Or were they?

The seats were way too big for them, and the controls on all three sides of them were too far to reach. Anyway, who could tell what all those buttons and dials and little monitors, flashing numbers, and graphs were even for?

"Maybe there's an instruction manual somewhere," Peter said.

"Maybe we should leave," Willy said.

They could sneak out without anyone noticing. Or hide in a closet and wait for the real astronauts. His guts twisted with fear. Or maybe it was just some gas.

His butt blew a little trumpet blast.

A voice crackled from a speaker. "What's that you just said, mission crew?"

"Uh, nothing," Willy said, coughing a little to disguise his voice.

A face appeared on a video screen. It was Mister Chan, the man who'd escorted them in the hall!

"I didn't see you enter the capsule," Chan said. "You guys strapped in?"

Willy and Peter looked at each other and gulped.

"Uh, booger that," Peter said.

"I think the word's *Roger*," Willy whispered.

The hamster started squeaking and rolling around the floor.

"What's that noise?" Chan said.

"Nothing," Peter said. "The chair's squeaking, needs oil."

"How come you're both sitting so low in your seats?" Chan said.

Another voice came on: *"Booster clamps clear. Ready to commence final countdown. Ten..."*

Willy pressed back in his seat. He couldn't believe what was happening. A couple hours ago he'd been lying on the living room couch, eating and farting and watching TV.

"Nine..."

And now he was inside a real space rocket about to fly all the way to the

Moon. No way out now; might as well have fun.

"Wait a sec," Chan said.

"Eight..."

Something moved in front of Willy. A little camera above the control panel seemed to be zooming in on them.

"Seven..."

Willy's whole body tingled with excitement. No, actually, it tingled because he had to pee. Real bad. He twisted in his seat.

"Six..."

He could hold it in. Sure. He'd held it in a million times in school. Only wet his pants once—*No, don't think about that!*

"Five..."

"What the—??" Chan said.

"Four..."

On the monitor, Chan's face turned white. "Commander Major is here right next to me. Then who the heck—"

"*Three...*"

"—are these kids?" The engine noise roared louder. The space capsule shook. Willy squeezed his knees together.

"*Two...*"

"Stop the countdown! Terminate launch!" Chan screamed.

"*One...*"

"What do you mean it's too—"

With a powerful lurch, the rocket began to move.

Willy was squashed back in his seat as though he weighed a thousand pounds.

He felt an electric thrill c o u r s e t h r o u g h his body.

He also felt warm liquid run down his leg and pool inside his space suit boots.

CHAPTER 7

Space Boogers

Willy couldn't believe it – they were up in space, floating in zero gravity!

Of course, so were a couple hundred nacho corn chips and some little black pellets which looked suspiciously like hamster poop.

They drifted through the air, devouring the chips with bean dip, while Chan interrogated them from Mission Control.

"Who the heck are you? How am I supposed to explain this to Mission Control leaders? I mean, how did you even get inside the space capsule?"

"You led us there," Peter said.

He told the story—well, the part of the story where Chan brought them from the auditorium and led them to the elevator. "Want us to explain to your supervisor?"

"Oh, you are in deep, deep trouble," Chan said.

"Actually, *you're* in deep trouble."

Willy and Peter laughed and gave each other a high five, which sent them sailing to opposite sides of the capsule.

Willy switched off the speakers, leaving Chan with his mouth flapping and fist waving in silence.

Now that they'd finished all the corn chips and bean dip, it was time to run the experiment that the whole world was waiting to see. They took positions side-by-side at the back of the capsule.

Willy's gut rumbled.

Peter's belly gurgled.

"Ready for countdown?" Peter said.

"Roger that," Willy replied.

They pulled down their pants and counted:

"Three...

Two...

One..."

FFFFFF–*blooooooorp-p-p!*

Willy jetted through the air, spewing dense green butt fumes, on a straight collision course with the windshield.

Just in the nick of time, he tightened one butt cheek, making a sharp left turn past the main control panel.

Peter zipped overhead, leaving a gray-

yellowish trail behind him.

Willy spun downward into a twisting loop, farting a perfect green figure-8 in the air before he ran out of fart power. In the zero-gravity environment, he kept smacking heads with Peter.

They gagged at the stench. That was a lot of fart for such a small place.

"Maybe we should open a window." Willy plugged his nose to hold back a sneeze. This gave him another idea for an experiment.

Willy sniffed and snorted and cleared his throat until his whole head felt like it was filled with mucus, then waited a minute to let the snot thicken.

"Watch this," he told Peter.

Pressing one nostril, he blew out the other. Gooey yellow boogers flowed from his nose while Willy spun through the air.

A long stringy worm of snot spelled out his name in perfect cursive letters:

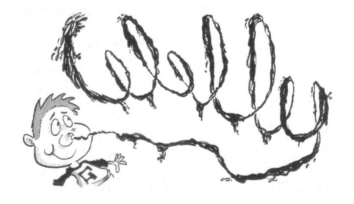

"Awesome," Peter said.

The tail of the *Y* stuck to a circuit panel. Sparks flew. Maybe this wasn't such a good idea. Willy positioned himself in front of the *W,* and slurped the whole thing into his mouth, until every slimy string was gone.

"Eeeuw!" Peter said.

"I second that *Eeeuw!*" Chan's voice said. He must have remotely turned the sound back on. "You guys do realize that you're on live video for the entire planet to see, right?"

"Of course," Peter said. "We're doing this in the name of science."

"I just spoke to the top brass. You guys are in deep, deep doo-doo. Now, sit down and pay attention so we can teach you how to pilot this thing. I want you back on Earth alive, so I can beat your smelly little butts."

Willy thought maybe that was a good idea—not the butt beating, but the part about returning alive. Once he and Peter settled into their seats, the lesson began.

Chan cleared his throat. "Okay, let's start with Newton's Laws of Motion."

"Sounds like school," Willy said, sticking his finger in his throat.

"Newton tootin'!" Peter said. He cut a loud, sharp fart.

"This is going to be one long trip to the Moon," Chan said.

CHAPTER 8
School's Out

Willy thought that flying an actual space capsule would be like living inside a real-life computer game, except without evil alien starships.

But by day two, Willy and Peter both realized that space travel was actually pretty boring. It was mainly sitting, or floating, around (though Willy was still a teeny bit worried about evil aliens).

And speaking of games, despite all the computer equipment on board, there wasn't a single one, not even a lousy tile-matching app! Unless they were on the computer that the hamster destroyed when he chewed a wire somewhere.

In fact, the only one who seemed to be enjoying himself was Squeaky, spinning around everywhere in his hamster ball.

Peter spent his time picking scabs off his leg and making them into little solar systems. But Willy had nothing to do except study.

Between the lessons from Mission Control and the science experiments they were supposed to do in space, it was feeling a bit too much like school. Chan even ordered Willy to sit in the corner after he threw spitwads at the camera.

But the worst part was the food. It took only one day to polish off all the good stuff: brownies, chocolate pudding cake, some cookies, and candy-coated peanuts.

Which left them now with the gross desserts like bread pudding, plus a whole lot of stuff that no self-respecting kid would eat, like cauliflower. Bleh!

"Dude, I'm hungry," Willy said.

"Me too," Peter said.

"Me three," Willy said. "Let's look one more time."

But all they found was the same as before: vacuum-packed sliced carrots. How disgusting can you get? Creamed spinach that looked like frog vomit.

Tofu? Who were they kidding? Not even grownups ate that glop!

"Look at this. What's it remind you of?" Peter squeezed out a packet of meatloaf in front of his mouth so it looked like he was puking.

"Yuck! You're disgusting," Willy said.

"And you're gonna eat it!" Peter rolled up the meat and pitched it at Willy.

Willy grabbed a sausage and batted the meat ball away. It bounced off the main dashboard and splattered all over the ceiling.

Willy tore open a package of beef ravioli and flung them one at a time at Peter, who fought back with shrimp cocktail, then strangled a package of mashed potatoes and green beans until it burst.

Half the mess got stuck in Willy's hair, while the rest was sucked into an air filter.

Willy returned fire with candied yams, laughing each time a gooey orange blob stuck to the walls with a squishy *floomp*.

"Hold on, we gotta video this," Willy said. He turned on his phone camera, and the intergalactic food fight resumed.

By the time they heard the hysterical voice from Mission Control, half the spacecraft's food decorated the walls and instrument panels. Peter stuck his finger through a lump of scrambled eggs to press the call answer button.

"What in blazes are you doing?" Chan demanded.

"Um, just sorting out lunch." Peter showed him the one promising thing they'd discovered: bean enchiladas, which looked great until they saw the label: *Reduced flatulence.*

"What's that about?" Peter asked.

"Use your brain," Chan said. "That's so you don't suffocate the rest of the crew."

"What's the point of eating beans, then?"

Willy was exhausted. He leaned back in his seat and felt a lump on his back. It was cold slab of marinated chicken. The control panel in front of him was like a painter's palette of multi-colored goop.

"Maybe we ought to clean up this mess," he said.

"Where we gonna put it?" Peter said.

"Didn't you see the garbage chamber? We just shoot it outside."

Willy's job was to scrape sticky, slimy mush and lumps and blobs off the windows.

Without thinking, he licked some off his fingers. Whoa! Tuna casserole mixed with pea soup and raspberry yogurt didn't taste too bad!

"Try this," he told Peter.

"Good stuff," Peter said. "Try what I got over here."

They made sandwiches of waffles

and beef stroganoff and butterscotch pudding.

"This is rather decent," Willy said.

Their stomachs had a different opinion. Willy's guts twisted as if someone was wringing out a rag inside him. Peter sounded like a thunderstorm was raging in his belly.

"Tea time over, gentlemen," said Chan. "Time to study orbital vector physics. For that I've brought in a specialist from Mission Control, Professor Fanny Frankentush."

Her hair was chimpanzee color. She had tiny eyes and a tight, puckered mouth.

"Good afternoon. I hope you young men are having an excellent learning experience up in space."

"We sure are," Peter said. "Want to see the Moon?"

She gave a pinched little smile. "Certainly."

Peter pulled down his pants and pointed his naked butt at the camera.

"Very funny," the lady professor said. "If you'll kindly open your text—"

PFFTHWLOOOORT!

An explosive fart shot Peter across the space capsule. It was answered by a juicy, disgusting *THWEEEP-P-P-P-BLARRRRGH* from Willy, spinning him like a pinwheel through the air.

The chimp-colored lady professor covered her mouth like she was sick. She muttered angrily to Chan, then disappeared from the screen. School was out for today.

Peter squeezed the reduced flatulence enchilada into the garbage chamber, then Willy pressed the lever to project it out into space.

Everything was once again all right with the universe.

CHAPTER 9

The Kids in the Moon

At last they were orbiting the Moon. Craters and boulders passed below.

"Whoa, that's a lot of green cheese," Peter said.

Willy rubbed his eyes. "You really think the Moon is made of green cheese?"

"Put it this way. We've just sat through about two zillion science lessons. Did they ever mention even once that it *isn't* made of green cheese?"

"Wow, you're right!" Willy squeezed his face to the glass. "It doesn't look very green, though."

"Don't you get it? That's the crust," Peter said. "Like those cheese wheels, where you peel off the wax first."

Willy smacked his lips. "Can't wait to cook up a bowl of macaroni and green cheese."

Peter sat in the Commander's seat and pressed the call button. "Hello? Mission Control dude? You there? We're at the Moon. Tell us how to land this thing."

Chan's smiling face formed on the screen. Wait a sec... *smiling?* Something was wrong here.

"Oh, really? Since when do you need my help? You already know how to land on the Moon."

Chan leaned into the camera until all they saw were angry lips and teeth.

"Or you would, if you'd paid attention to a single word I've said over the past five days, instead of belching and farting and picking your noses."

"Those aren't farts, those are descriptions of your face," Peter said. "Just talk us through it."

"Oh, you'd like that, huh? Just talk you through it. Like I've been talking through your empty little skulls this whole time. Well, here's your chance to put those burpy brains to the test, you little twits."

Willy's lip trembled. He let out a great big sob. They were so close to the Moon, so close to making history, so close to some tasty-looking cheese.

"Don't cry. Please don't cry." Chan sighed. "All right, I'll help just this once. But next time you visit another planet, you're on your own."

"So what do I do?" Peter said.

"Not you," Chan said. "Your brother there."

"But I'm Mission Commander!" Peter protested.

"Sorry, that's the price of being a rude little snot. Little brother sails the ship. No? See you, then. Over and—"

"Okay!" Peter blurted. With a nasty sneer, he blasted a fart into the Commander's seat cushion, then traded places with Willy.

"Okie dokie," Chan said. "See that big red button? Yeah? Put your finger on it and—*Ha! Fooled you!* That's the self-destruct button. *Kidding!* Press that green one next to it when I tell you. That's for the reverse thrusters."

Willy's belly tightened, his finger trembled on the button. "What happens if I push it too soon?"

"You over-shoot the Moon and head out forever into space."

"And if I push it too late?"

"You crash land in a pile of crushed metal. Got me?"

"Y-y-y-y-y–" Willy's teeth chattered so hard he couldn't finish the word.

"All right. On your mark...get set..." Chan said, "...three...two...one..."

Willy swallowed hard. His guts felt like they might explode.

"GO!"

Willy pressed the button, but no matter how hard he jabbed, it wouldn't go down!

"It's stuck!" Willy cried.

"It's glued in place by dried blueberry pie filling and mushroom soup," Peter said. "We're gonna crash!"

"You're gonna crash!" Chan said.

The Moon's surface loomed larger. "We've got to dissolve it!" Willy cried.

He stood on his seat and unzipped his pants. A little squirt was all it took.

Sparks flew, and a couple nearby switches started smoking. But the gunk around the green button bubbled and fizzed. But while zipping, Willy's finger got stuck in his fly.

"Press it!" Willy ordered Peter.

"No way. I'm not touching your wee. I'd rather crash!"

"Argh!" Willy dove from his seat and rammed his nose onto the reverse thruster button.

The space capsule shuddered. Engines fired. Gears turned, hydraulic pumps hissed. The Moon's surface came at them more gently.

Willy dropped back into his seat, gripping the armrests like bird claws. He didn't know if he was dizzy from fear and excitement or the smell coming from the control panel.

The rocket thrusters quit. Landing

gear struck the surface with a soft, squishy *sploop!*

Sploop? Shouldn't it have been more like *whack* or at least *boing?*

"That was actually good thinking, Commander," Peter said.

"Thanks, Lieutenant," Willy said.

They gave each other high fives, then announced to the world:

"Greetings, Earthlings, from the first kids on the Moon!"

CHAPTER 10

One Small Toot

Of course, they immediately started fighting over who got to take the first step on the lunar surface.

"Older ones exit first, like at school final bell," Peter said, scrambling into his spacesuit while knee-kicking Willy away from the door.

"Younger ones first, like at school assembly," Willy said, fastening his helmet with one hand while punching Peter with the other.

They pushed and tugged and kicked, and would have bitten if they weren't wearing helmets, until Peter finally said, "Tell you what. We'll go together. I've got a little speech, and you can lead off. Fair?"

Willy released the hammer hold on his brother's neck. "I dunno. Fair, I guess."

"Okay, when I raise my thumb, you cut your loudest trumpet-blower fart."

"That's the speech?"

"That's your part," Peter said. "Ready?"

He opened the hatch. Together they stepped onto the top rung of the exit ladder. Peter did a thumbs-up toward the outside camera.

Willy spread his cheeks and let rip the first fart ever heard on the Moon.

"That's one small *toot* for man," Peter recited, then blew a zinging foghorn. "One giant fart for mankind."

Together they jumped.

In the Moon's low gravity they floated
down, down, down, until their feet struck
something solid.

Or not exactly solid.

Actually, it was kind of gummy.

Willy raised one boot. Thick goo stuck to the bottom. He reached down to feel the surface.

His fingers went right through.

It felt like macaroni cheese sauce. He scooped up a handful. Peter dug both gloves in and gathered up a big wad of the stuff.

Back inside the landing vehicle, they removed their helmets and studied the glop they'd collected. It was cream-colored, with little yellow-gray chunks.

Peter stuck his nose close. "You're not gonna believe what it smells like."

Willy sniffed and didn't believe it. "Should we taste it?"

"You first."

"No, you first."

"No, you," Peter said.

"Oh yeah, mister smartypants?" Willy

84

said. "You're all, 'the Moon is made of green cheese' and now you're scared to try it? Well, I'm not scared."

He dipped a finger into the substance and pressed it lightly to his tongue.

"Huh?" He tasted again.

"It is indeed onion dip."

Peter shoved his finger in and sucked the whole thing off.

"You're right! We just made the biggest scientific discovery of the century! The Moon isn't made of green cheese—it's made of onion dip!"

Then Peter slapped his forehead. "Oh, man, this is terrible!"

"What?"

"We've found the biggest hoard of onion dip in the whole universe! Everyone knows the Universal Law of Snacking: you can't eat onion dip without rippled potato chips!"

Chan's voice surprised them from the overhead monitor: "Open the floor panel between the command seats."

Peter bounded over and unlatched the panel, revealing a compartment with at least a hundred jumbo sized bags of rippled potato chips.

Willy spun toward the screen. "You mean...you *knew?*"

"People have been here before, you know," Chan said.

Peter stammered, "Then why–?"

"We had to keep it secret. Otherwise, the Russians, and especially the French, would be crowding the Moon's surface with onion dip mines."

"But what about the moon rocks that astronauts brought back in the past? Weren't those real?" Peter said, as he ripped open a bag of chips. He and Willy feasted on fresh, delicious lunar onion dip while Chan continued.

"Oh, those. You see, early on, the top onion dip companies heard rumors. They got together to build their own private rockets, with plans to exploit the Moon. We had to convince them the rumors were false.

"Those moon rocks? Bits of broken concrete from a demolished parking garage. Slipped them in the space capsules after they returned to Earth."

"So who actually knows?" Willy asked with his mouth full.

Chan took a deep breath, and said, "Top Lunar Program management. The original astronauts. And now you guys. And the President, which is why...never mind."

"Never mind what?" Peter said. "What's the real reason for this mission?"

"We didn't want to do it," Chan said. "But the President's having this potluck barbecue party with the Russians and wants to show off with about twenty gallons—um. Sorry, I can't reveal any more. Don't you breathe a word of any of this!" Chan signed off.

Willy and Peter spent the rest of the day hopping around the Moon's surface, having onion dip cannonball fights and sliding down onion dip slopes, all of which felt really weird in the

Moon's light gravity. Finally, they filled a couple buckets with Moon dip, went back inside, and scarfed it down with rippled potato chips. Less than a minute after swallowing each mouthful, their tummies would rumble, and out would shoot farts of such aggressive force and nose-dissolving stench that they were left choking for breath.

"This stuff is awesome!" Willy wheezed.

"If only we had orange soda," Peter panted.

Willy was enjoying a long, growling fart, when suddenly he froze. He stood up and looked around. "Hey, have you seen Squeaky?"

Peter got to his feet. They searched under every seat and cabinet, every compartment, every crawl space, every drawer.

"Do you suppose...?" Willy said.

He pressed his nose to the window and scanned the glaring creamy surface of the Moon.

At last his eye caught onto a squiggly line in the gooey ground, winding around craters and disappearing into the distance. A line that could only have been made by a hamster ball.

CHAPTER 11

Dark Side of the Moon

Willy placed an urgent call to Mission Control.

"We need the Moon Buggy! Tell us how to use it, quick!"

"You mean the Lunar Rover?" Chan rubbed his eyes like he'd just woken from a nap.

"Whatever," Willy said. "How do we unpack it and drive it?"

"Either of you guys have a license?"

Peter and Willy gawked at each other.

Who needed a driver's license on the Moon? "Just tell us how to set it up," Peter said. "We're in kind of a hurry."

"Mind telling me what's the urgent need?" Chan picked up a cup of coffee and took a long, deep sip.

"Our hamster got loose."

The monitor suddenly filled with brown, runny liquid and the sound of Chan gagging. "What. Hamster?"

Peter told him the whole story, except the part about Squeaky's poop floating around and getting into the machinery.

Chan wiped his camera lens. His shirt was a mess of coffee stains. "You're telling me a hamster has been running loose the entire voyage?"

"Anyway, he hasn't damaged much, except a few wires, which is maybe why one of the computers died, and maybe he got into the breakfast food, and maybe chewed up a couple control switches, but—"

"Oh, you two are so dead," Chan's lips hardly moved over his red-faced sneer.

"When you get back to Earth you are both dead as doorknobs. Deader. I mean,  you'll *wish* you were doorknobs. You'll wish you never were born. When I get my claws on you, I'll—"

"Yeah, yeah, okay, okay," Peter broke in. "Um, the Lunar Rover, remember? We've got a hamster to rescue."

Chan sighed. "Try Storage Module C. The manuals are in a slot on the door. Meantime, I've got to download some torture instructions. Oh, you guys are mincemeat!"

The screen went blank.

Putting together the Lunar Rover turned out to be easier than some of the fancy Lego sets they'd owned. In the end it was the coolest-looking thing either of them had ever built.

They just had to take loads of selfies with their phones, which luckily ran out of power and died. Otherwise, they might have forgotten what they were supposed to be doing.

Then they fought over who got to drive.

"I'm better at driving amusement park bumper cars," Willy said.

"Yeah, well I'm seven levels above you in Grand Stolen Auto."

"Let's draw straws," Willy said.

"What straws?" Peter said. "How about who farts the longest?"

"That's fair."

Since they'd eaten nothing but potato chips and onion dip all day, the contest got off to a quick start.

Willy flexed his stomach muscles, adjusted his butt, and whistled out a high-pitched squealie that went on for so long that he got dizzy from lack of oxygen inside his space suit.

"78.3 seconds," Peter announced. "Now me."

Peter showed off by farting the theme

tunes of two science fiction movie series, for which he claimed extra points. Despite that, his fart lasted only 76.9 seconds.

He tossed Willy the key.

Since no road trip is complete without snacks, they stuffed the Rover with bags of rippled potato chips, then set off on their lunar journey.

Willy did his best to follow the hamster ball's trail. Bouncing over rough ground, rumbling through wide, bowl-shaped craters, all made his stomach queasy.

He was driving up a steep ridge, when he blasted out a rancid, blustery fart. The smell was so sharp it made his nostrils itch.

"Ah...ah..."

He needed so badly to scratch his nose and stop himself from...from...

He sneezed so violently his head snapped back. Willy couldn't see a thing through the thick snot and undigested chips and onion dip all over his visor.

Without thinking, he took his hands off the wheel to wipe the glass, though of course it was all on the inside.

"Slow down! Turn left!" Peter yelled. "We're going over a cliff!"

Willy's helmet speaker was gummed

up with phlegm, so he couldn't hear a thing. Anyway, he was too busy screaming his lungs out.

Peter grabbed the wheel, but it was too late.

They were flying through empty space.

On the positive side, Peter's newest shriek of terror cleared Willy's helmet speakers.

BAM! They struck the surface. Though, this being the Moon, it wasn't exactly a *bam*; more like *boomph.*

Willy used his nose to wipe a clear spot in the glass.

They were at the bottom of a deep crater, where it was black as a moonless night. Or earthless. He searched the sky, but Earth was nowhere to be seen. Even the radio connection to Mission Control had gone silent.

"We're on the dark side of the Moon!" Peter said.

"And we've lost the hamster trail."

Willy began to cry, which was actually useful, since he could clean the visor by shaking his head and splashing it with tears.

"But we found something else," Peter said.

Way over in the middle of the crater was a strange-looking structure: black and shiny in the weak starlight, shaped like a short, wide, upside-down ice cream cone.

A thick cable rose from the cone's peak and continued up into space, connected way overhead to...

Willy stopped breathing. No, this couldn't be real. He tapped his brother's shoulder, but Peter was staring straight up, too.

At a big, scary alien starship.

CHAPTER 12
Breath of Fresh Air

The heavily armed alien spaceship hovered in space above the Moon.

It looked like a giant spider, with glowing quantum engines on each leg, and weapons pointing everywhere, which Willy recognized from comic books as Photon Plasma Beam Cannons.

"We better get out of here," Willy said.

"No way!" Peter said. "We need selfies with aliens. Then Mission Control will call us heroes instead of being mad."

"I'm sure they know about it already."

"How could they? This is the dark side of the Moon. You can't see it from Earth. We've just made the biggest discovery in human history. We'll be legends!"

"Let's just take some pictures from here first, and—oh, poop-dee-doo!"

Both phones were dead, of course, after wasting their batteries on about two hundred and fifty selfies with the Lunar Rover.

"Here's what we'll do," Peter said. "We'll go back to the Lander, recharge batteries, inform Mission Control, and—um. Uh oh."

Willy sensed dark forms looming behind him.

He turned.

He gulped.

He and Peter said:

"*AAAAAAAAAAAHHHHHHHHHH!*"

Two creatures which looked like giant green lima beans stared back through three huge yellow eyes.

Willy tried to start the Lunar Rover, but green shoots snaked from the creatures' bodies like sprouting plants, looped around Willy and Peter, and plucked them right out of their seats.

A moment later they were soaring over the ground, roped to their captors, who spewed blue exhaust from their rear ends. These creatures used fart power to fly!

They flew through an opening in the cone-shaped ground structure, then released Willy and Peter inside, dropping them on the floor.

The interior was one big brightly-lit chamber, filled with lima bean aliens and strange machines. In the center, a huge rotating corkscrew slowly drilled into the ground.

Willy lay on the floor, too scared to move or even breathe, as more aliens gathered around him and Peter.

We're dead, Willy thought. *They're going to eat us, or cut us up for experiments.*

He blubbered and snorted and sobbed and squeaked.

Wait a second, those weren't his squeaks. They sounded familiar, though.

A hamster crawled onto his foot. Squeaky! But where was his hamster ball?

Peter sat up. He undid his helmet clamps, signaling Willy to do the same. "Squeaky can breathe in here. That means so can we!"

He was right. It was like inhaling pure, sweet mountain air, fresher than the stuff in their oxygen tanks.

The aliens stood around belching at each other. Either they were more immature than Earth first graders, or that was what their language sounded like.

Peter bent over in obvious pain. "What do I do? I gotta fart so bad after all that onion dip. When they smell it, they're going to kill us for sure."

But it was too late. Peter's face pinched up, then he tooted so loud they could have heard it on Mars.

The aliens instantly stopped talking. One of them grabbed Peter and pulled him out of his space suit. The alien raised Peter to its mouth.

Peter fought like a wildcat. "It's gonna eat me! Help!"

"Try farting in its mouth!" Willy said.

Peter ripped a loud one, but the alien only bit down harder.

"Help! It's sucking my butt!"

Willy ran at Peter's tormentor, but an alien tentacle caught and dragged him out of his space suit, then held him to its lips just like Peter. Willy was so frightened he let out a blistering fart.

Was he imagining things? The creature was drinking it in!

The way his and Peter's aliens wobbled a little, Willy could have sworn they seemed drunk.

The two big beans slapped branches, like they were high-fiving each other. Willy would have laughed if his life weren't in danger.

Or was it?

Willy's captor passed him to another alien, which wrapped its lips around Willy's butt, then tapped Willy's belly. It wanted Willy to fart! He gave the alien what gas he had left.

The alien seemed to sigh with happiness, then set Willy back on the floor. Peter's alien put him down too. The other giant beans chattered in their belch language.

Another creature, taller than the rest and a darker shade of green, lumbered forward and extended a tentacle.

"We not hurt you," said a deep, gargly voice. It was speaking to them. In English!

"Where are you from? What do you want from us?" Peter said.

"We from Planet Uranus. We breathe methane. You make finest methane in all universe."

"Is he saying what I think he's saying?" Willy whispered.

"Yup. They breathe farts. And think ours are the best."

"Then I don't get it," Willy said. "Why is this place filled with oxygen?"

A deep rumbling noise came from inside the tall alien's rubbery green body. It built into a burble, rising faster and higher until it sounded like a trombone orchestra.

A fat blue cloud shot from the alien's rear end, blanketing Willy and Peter before they could escape.

They covered their mouths and tried fanning the mist away. Then, without thinking, Willy sniffed.

Just to make sure, he sniffed again.

It was the sweetest-smelling air that had ever entered his nose—like a flowery meadow beside the sea, with a hint of fresh-baked bread and movie theater buttered popcorn.

He gulped in deep breaths. Peter's eyes bulged out in wonder, then he did the same.

"Wow, we're breathing alien farts," Peter said. "I guess that's how our farts smell to them."

Willy looked up at the tall alien, who he guessed was their leader. "But what are you doing here?"

"I tell after eat," the alien leader said.

"No way are you eating us!" Willy tried to run, but an alien tentacle lassoed his ankle and tripped him to the floor.

"Not you." The alien leader pointed to the ground. "Eat onion dip."

"By itself?" Peter said.

"Of course not," the alien said. "Universal Law of Snacking: can only eat onion dip with rippled *kablooga* chips. Come try."

Peter nodded to Willy. "I think we'd better cooperate."

They sat in a circle with the aliens. The *kablooga* chips tasted like stiff shredded cardboard. In other words, no worse than the 'organic health snacks' they were always forced to eat at home.

"There's something I need to know first," Peter said. "How do you say the name of your planet? Is it *Urine-Us* or *Your Anus?* Either way it's pretty hilarious."

"You think funny?" The alien leader sneered. "You should hear what *Earth* sound like in our language."

He unleashed a gnarly, gargling belch that sounded sort of like *"Uuuurrrrrrpthhhhhhhh."*

The other aliens slapped their sides and popped a lot of short burps, which was clearly their way of laughing. They laughed so hard several of them let out big blue saxophone-like farts, which smelled to Willy like fresh-baked cherry pies.

The leader clapped his tentacles. Snack time over.

"Now I tell story why Uranus mission to Earth Moon."

CHAPTER 13

The Uranian Plot

The alien leader released what might have been an ordinary burp, or might have been orders for everyone to be quiet and listen.

He introduced himself, though his name was an unpronounceable, throat-rattling belch.

"We are sent here by our president, the Great Big Pupu Head in Uranus."

"We have a President like that, too," Peter said.

"Quiet! Only one Great Big Pupu Head! He appoint me number one Big Fat Pupu Face."

"Then who are these guys?" Willy asked.

The Big Fat Pupu Face pointed to a pair of his companions.

"My chief officers, Pipi Face and Pipi Pants. In charge of workers we call Little Pipi's."

Willy gulped back a laugh, which set loose a little rump ripper. The Big Fat Pupu Face leaned over and slurped every foul drop into his lungs.

The alien leader whistled with pleasure and continued.

"On Planet Uranus, atmosphere is hydrogen, helium, and methane. We breathe methane. But only one source of fresh methane on whole planet: Uranus cow-snail farts! Everywhere billions of cow-snails, all day eat and fart, fart and eat, refill atmosphere with methane. Everybody happy."

"What do they eat?" Peter said.

The alien leader, annoyed at the interruption, turned his back on Peter, blew a disgusting-sounding blue fart that smelled like fresh mountain air, before answering: "Dingleberries."

"You have dingleberries on Uranus," Peter said.

"What I just told you!" the alien leader barked.

"No, I meant you really have...oh, never mind." Peter shrugged.

"Cow-snails eat only dingleberries,

fart methane," the Big Fat Pupu Face explained.

"What's that have to do with our Moon?" Willy asked.

"*Uuuurrrrrrpthhhhhhh* boy try listen." This triggered burpy-laughs from the Big and Little Pipi's. The Big Fat Pupu Face belched for silence.

"Now too much people on Uranus, fart oxygen all day. Too many factories, too many drive Uranus car, need too many power plants burn dingleberry wood, pollute air with oxygen. Make bad, bad climate change!

"Worse: climate change is making dingleberries all sick and dying. No dingleberries, no cow-snail farts. Soon no methane to breathe."

He spread his branch-like arms. "Then we discover cow-snails also eat onion dip. So we come to Earth Moon."

So that was it—the aliens planned to fill a ship with onion dip and carry it back to Uranus!

Peter raised his hand.

"Okay, let me get this straight. The Great Big Pupu Head in Uranus had trouble with dingleberries, so he called you a Big Fat Pupu Face, and you told Pipi Face and Pipi Pants to put their Little Pipi's on the Moon and dig up a ship load of snail fart food."

"Correct, Earth boy, except for one

thing. We take whole Moon. Take you, too."

Everything became clearer now: the giant corkscrew, slowly cutting deeper into the Moon's surface; the cable attached to the huge powerful spacecraft. They wanted to drag the Moon out of Earth's orbit and tow it all the way to Uranus.

"Wait a minute!" Willy said. "Uranus has its own moons. Why not use those instead?"

The Big Fat Pupu Face put on a sad look, if big-eyed beans could even look sad.

"Unfortunately, our moons made of pistachio ice cream. Nobody in whole universe likes pistachio ice cream. Even cow-snails spit out."

Willy nodded. That made sense. But the rest didn't. He cried to Peter, "They're going to steal our Moon!"

"Cool," Peter said.

"What are you talking about?"

"I mean, not that I'm necessarily in favor of letting them steal the Moon, but if they were able to pull it off, it would be kind of awesome to watch."

"You—!" Willy was at a loss for words. How could Peter even think such a thing? He leaned close to his brother and whispered, "We need to stop them. Our entire planet is depending on us!"

But Peter had a weird, far-away look. "I've been thinking," he said.

"Uh-oh," Willy muttered to himself. Every time Peter started thinking, it ended up with both of them in even bigger trouble.

Peter put his hand on Willy's shoulder. "Pupu Face said he wants us to go with them. Maybe we should."

"Are you crazy?"

"No. Think about it," Peter said. "Remember they claimed our farts were the finest in the whole universe? We'll be rock stars on Uranus! Instead of being punished for farting in public like at home, people on Uranus will line up and pay big bucks to sniff our butts. We can bottle the stuff. We'll get rich off it! We'll live like kings!"

"I don't know..." Willy said.

"Think of the other advantages! No more math homework. No tidying our rooms or taking out the garbage or visits to smoochy Aunt Bertha. No more being dragged to the mall to try on shoes, or being forced to eat peas. And best of all...no icky kindergarten pageants to sit through ever again!"

Willy had to admit that last argument was fairly convincing. But to leave Earth forever? Think of all the things he'd miss, like... Uh. Like...

Certainly not Jimmy Crawford, the school bully. Or Ms. Watkins, his history teacher who hated his guts. There hadn't been a decent kids' TV show in a long time, and none of the new games coming out was anything special. There actually wasn't much worth missing!

Anyway, did they have a choice? The Uranians weren't about to let them go and warn Earth, plus they had nothing to fight with. And yet...

"I won't do it!" Willy reached into his pocket and held up the key to the Lunar Rover. "I'm leaving!"

Peter turned his back and walked away.

"Fine. Go back to Earth yourself."

CHAPTER 14

Home Alone

Willy couldn't believe what was happening.

His brother stood across the room laughing and joking with the Big Fat Pupu Face, while the other Uranians continued working on stealing the Moon. Alien tools clanged and clattered around the giant turning corkscrew. Something twinkled like a sparkler.

Tears covered Willy's cheeks. Snot flowed over his lips. He was so upset he didn't even eat it.

He could get furious at Peter. He could accuse Peter of being stubborn. But that would violate their sworn policy to always blame everything on their little sister. So, instead, he thought:

If only Skyler weren't a sheep in the kindergarten play, he and his brother wouldn't have been forced into stealing space suits and running off to the Moon, to be captured by fart-sucking alien lima beans, and Peter wouldn't be spending the rest of his life stuck in Uranus.

Now Willy had to figure out how to fly back to Earth all by himself. He'd never see his big brother again.

Worse, it would be just him and his dumb little sister, the one who caused this mess in the first place.

Peter ran over and grabbed Willy's shoulders.

"You've got to come to Uranus! I was just talking to them about a business plan. We'll package our farts, make them into perfumes, air fresheners, stuff like that. Sell them all over the planet, even Jupiter and Neptune. We'll be stinking rich! Ha ha! Get it?

"Maybe that's what we'll call our brand: Stinking Rich Fragrances. Or how about Flatulence Number Five?"—he said it in a French accent: *flawt-you-lawns.* "Come on, it'll be so much better if we do it together."

"I want to go home." Willy picked up his space suit.

"Yeah, well, don't say I didn't offer you. One day when I'm living in my mansion on Uranus, and you're just sitting there picking your nose down on Earth…"

"If I get back to Earth."

New tears welled up in Willy's eyes.

"My oxygen tank is nearly down to zero. How am I supposed to make it back to the lunar lander?"

Peter examined the tank, then snapped his fingers. "I know."

He ran back to the Uranian leader, who returned with one of the Little Pipi's.

The Little Pipi scooped up a heaping wad of onion dip with a *kablooga* chip, wolfed them down, then immediately bent over. The Big Fat Pupu Face picked up Willy's oxygen tank.

Oh no, gross, Willy thought. He wasn't really going to shove the tank in there, was he?

He was. That is, he did. And not just in, but all the way inside. Loud rumbling and grumbling, a spitter and a spatter. Muted horns blew a concert in the alien's gut, along with burbles and pops and what sounded like pigs squealing.

The Little Pipi clenched its butt and pushed.

"Eeuw," Willy said.

The oxygen tank slid out, sparkling clean. The gauge showed one hundred percent full!

It was time to say goodbye. Willy turned to shake his brother's hand, but Peter had already wandered off with his new alien friends. All Willy had to do now was find Squeaky.

He searched behind boxes and in dark corners. He worked his way to the giant corkscrew in the center of the room.

The hole it had drilled was so deep and so dark Willy couldn't see the bottom. A narrow board formed a dangerous-looking bridge across it. If Squeaky had fallen down there, he had no hope.

Peter and the Big Fat Pupu Face stood a few steps away, drinking a toast with blue-green liquid in strange cups. Peter swallowed his in one gulp, getting burps of approval from the other aliens.

Peter replied with a deep, long, bubbly belch of his own.

Every alien in the room froze. The

Uranian leader frowned deeply. His body looked like it was about to erupt, changing from green to red to fiery orange.

"How dare you talk about my mother that way!"

The Big Fat Pupu Face grabbed Peter by the neck and shook him like a rag doll, while the other aliens whipped him with their tentacles. Peter's hands clawed the air. His face went purple.

Willy leapt through the air and landed on the Big Fat Pupu Face's back. He pinched and punched and kicked the cold, slimy alien skin.

"Leave my brother alone, you ugly, stupid alien! Your mother is a—*burrrrp!*"

A tentacle flung him across the room. He came down hard—actually, not that hard in the Moon's low gravity—beside the giant corkscrew pit, its yawning darkness just an arm's length away.

The alien leader dropped Peter and lumbered in Willy's direction.

"Stop, or I'll—" Willy said.

"You'll what?" The Big Fat Pupu Face spun around and aimed his butt at Willy.

What's he going to do, fart oxygen in my face? Willy thought.

A supersonic jet-powered fart swept Willy over the edge of the corkscrew pit. Grabbing the side of the narrow bridge just in time, he was left holding on for dear life, dangling over the gaping hole.

A Little Pipi walked over with one of the strange sparklers Willy had seen earlier, and waved it behind the Uranian leader.

His fart turned into a flaming blowtorch.

The Big Fat Pupu Face belched through clenched teeth:

"Now you die."

CHAPTER 15

Dueling Gassers

The Uranian leader's flaming fart narrowed into a blue-hot fart-saber.

It jabbed and scorched Willy's fingers, loosening his grip. Below him lay nothing but blackness.

Peter, meanwhile, was tied up in the tentacles of two Little Pipis.

"You've got to fart your way out!" Peter yelled.

"I can't," Willy said. "There's nothing in my guts."

"Eat Moon onion dip!" Peter said.

It was useless advice, and they both knew it. Even in an emergency like this, it was against the Universal Law of Snacking to eat onion dip without chips.

The Big Fat Pupu Face slashed again and again with his fart-saber. Willy began to lose his grip.

"P-Peter, help!" Willy cried, holding on by a single hand. One small slip and he would fall to his doom.

"I've got it!" Peter shouted.

He rolled up his pant leg and carefully peeled off a scab so big, black, and ugly, it even grossed him out.

Peter's arm drew back, then with every fiber of strength, he spun the scab through the air, exclaiming:

"May the Flatulence be with you!"

Willy's free hand caught the flying scab. It was thick and lumpy, and gooey on one side—he fought the urge to vomit.

He reached over to the edge of the pit and shoveled up a small mountain of onion dip. But even then, he didn't immediately shove it in his mouth.

Eating his brother's scab would be the most disgusting thing he'd ever done in his life—well, except maybe the time he accidentally stepped in dog doo and tracked it all over the house, including on his sister's bed.

Just do it, he told himself.

He placed the scab on his tongue.

He gagged.

He chewed.

The scab turned out to be leathery, though crisp around the edges. It tasted like burnt cheese. But it was still gross.

He shut off his mind.

He swallowed.

Eww.

Powerful fizzing and foaming, like fireworks in his guts, wound down through the maze of his intestines. At last, he felt the tell-tale bloat, like balloons inflating inside his belly.

The fart burst out like a spouting whale. In the low gravity it gave the boost he needed to pull himself onto the bridge.

The alien's fart-saber scorched the bridge near Willy's feet.

Willy turned around, loosened his pants and aimed.

An epic fart shot through the air, touched the alien leader's sizzling weapon, and ignited into flame. Willy now had his own orange-hot fart-saber.

The Big Fat Pupu Face attacked with masterful moves, driving Willy backward to the middle of the rickety bridge, which bent and swayed over the corkscrew pit. It was all Willy could do to keep his balance and fight at the same time.

The Big Fat Pupu Face struck with an inside left. Willy parried with a low thrust. But the alien had the greater skill, attacking with a rapid series of jabs.

One swinging blow so narrowly missed his face that Willy lost control. His fart began to sputter. He was almost out of gas!

At last, Willy got in a lucky jab, scorching the alien's free tentacle in a little burst of green smoke. But rather than making the Uranian leader retreat, it sent him into a rage.

Willy dodged and ducked one ferocious thrust after another, driving him to within a few short steps of the churning corkscrew blade.

"Come on, Willy!" Peter jumped and waved his arms, while the Uranians belched support for their leader.

Willy's legs were losing strength. His fart gas was running dangerously low. He closed his eyes and remembered his brother's words:

May the Flatulence be with you.

He knew exactly the move he had to make.

His knees clamped together. His butt poised to strike his target at its very heart. Ready to unleash the deciding fart blast, he clenched his sphincter muscles, when he heard a sharp metallic snap that chilled him to the bone.

CHAPTER 16
War of the Worlds

It sounded like the barbed twang of a breaking guitar string.

Then another.

The Uranian leader heard it too. The duel came to a stop while Willy and the Big Fat Pupu Face teetered on the narrow bridge, craning their heads in search of the sound's source.

There it was again, just behind Willy—an ear-piercing metallic pop, followed by a long, whining *SPROING!*

The Big Fat Pupu Face trembled with fear. Willy turned to look.

The noise came from the cable attached to the giant corkscrew—the one running through the top of the structure and on up through space to the Uranian space ship. The cable that would tow the Moon to Uranus. That cable was made from hundreds of metal strings, all twisted together.

That cable was coming apart.

There it was again: one of the strings snapped. Now Willy saw why.

"Squeaky!"

The crazy little hamster perched on top of the corkscrew, nibbling away at the cable.

ka-BOING!

There went another strand.

The Big Fat Pupu Face pointed his fart-saber toward the unsuspecting hamster.

Willy had only a few seconds of intestinal gas left. Enough for one final flaming swing at the Uranian leader.

But what if he missed?

Willy bounced up and down on the rickety bridge, throwing the Big Fat Pupu Face off balance.

The alien belched furiously, slashing again and again at the hamster with his deadly flame, getting nearer each time.

Willy crouched low. With one mighty kick, he launched himself high into the air, his fart propelling him like a rocket.

PLINK! Another cable strand snapped.

Squeaky's sharp little teeth clamped onto the last remaining strand. A fart-saber jab singed his whiskers.

Willy squeezed everything he had into one absolutely final blast of gas, grabbing the hamster as he zoomed past. The bottomless dark pit loomed below. Would he make it to the other side?

May the Flatulence be with you.

One last little butt peep did the trick.

Willy tumbled down onto safe, solid ground.

The shrill whine of the cable's one remaining strand sounded like a giant slingshot stretching back and back.

The Big Fat Pupu Face belched orders. The Little Pipi's ran around like frightened Uranian chickens.

"Let's get out of here!" Willy shouted to Peter.

They jumped into their space suits and ran. Sitting beside the entrance was the missing hamster ball.

—*kerrrr...SNAP!!!*—

The cable broke. It spun toward the ceiling.

"Jump!" Willy cried.

They leaped out the door.

If the Moon had a real atmosphere, they might have heard a terrible ripping sound, as the entire Uranian base tore from the lunar surface, aliens and all, and tumbled end over end like one of those roll-up paper party horns, away up into space.

The Uranian starship fired its engines, but too late. The spinning mass of wire and metal pierced the ship like a bullet.

The spaceship shuddered. Its lights went out.

Then the only thing visible was a huge angry ball of orange smoke and debris.

It was the coolest fireworks display Willy had ever seen. A few flame bursts later, nothing remained of the Uranian mission other than a few sparkling embers drifting off toward the stars.

"Nobody's going to believe a single word of this," Peter said.

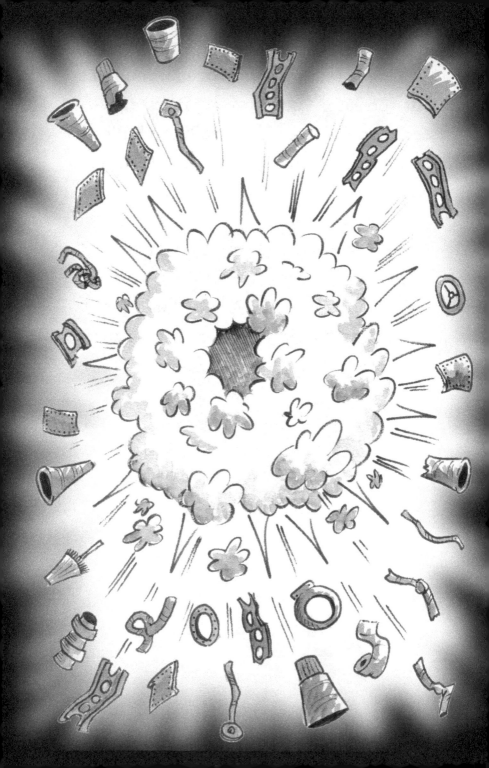

CHAPTER 17

Planet Gas

"I don't believe a single word of this," said a red-faced Mister Chan, spittle spraying from gritted teeth.

He pounded a fist on a messy stack of papers on his messy white desk in his plain white office in the stark white Mission Control headquarters.

Willy and Peter twisted in their seats on the other side of the desk. Their attempt to land the returning spacecraft in Siberia or the Sahara Desert, or anywhere as far as possible from Space Command, had failed when they'd spilled tropical punch all over the controls.

After splashing down right in the middle of a water fun park, they'd been delivered by helicopter directly to Chan's office.

"You've got to believe us. Cross my heart," Peter said. "There's life on Uranus."

"On my *what?*" Chan screeched.

"The planet, stupid," Peter said. "We discovered big-eyed beans from Uranus trying to steal the Moon to feed to flatulent cow-snails."

"And I stopped them with my burning fart-saber," Willy said. "Plus, our sister's hamster helped."

Chan tapped his fingertips together.

"Right. And I'm supposed to believe that. Prove it!"

"Sure, I'll prove it," Peter said. "Know how they say the name of our planet in their language?"

He drew in a deep breath, then belched loud enough to be heard three doors away:

"Uuuurrrrrrrpthhhhhhhh!"

Chan looked ready to explode. "Oh, you guys are dead. I mean, you were already dead before, but now you're much, much deader."

He picked up a thick stack of papers. "Know what this is? This is a list. Of every law, ordinance, regulation, and procedure you two have broken."

There were thousands. Chan pulled out a random page and read:

"Carrying an un-quarantined animal into space. Importing food from another planet without inspection. Improper use of official documents."

"We ran out of toilet paper," Willy said.

"And this," Chan flicked another paper stack, which was only a little bit thinner, "is a list of lost and broken materials, including one whole space capsule which has to be sold as playground equipment, plus two Extravehicular Mobility Units...."

"What are you talking about? We didn't destroy any space suits," Peter said.

"The amount of gas pooted inside those suits, our maintenance staff said they'll never get the smell out. They had to be incinerated."

Chan leaned across the desk into their faces. "You two are going to spend the rest of your lives in prison," Chan said. "As soon as I get your names."

Peter looked at Willy. Willy looked at Peter.

"You mean, we never told you?" Peter said.

Chan took out a piece of paper and a pen. He nodded at Willy. "You first."

Willy put his hand over his heart and said, "Frank N. Farter."

"And I'm his cousin, Yura Buttface," said Peter.

"Is that one or two T's?" Chan said.

He finished writing, then picked up the phone. "Hi. Send the National Security Team, please. I've got a Farter and a Buttface in need of hard labor."

"Wait a second!" Willy pressed the disconnect button on Chan's phone. "If we can really prove that we met aliens from Uranus"—he stopped to giggle along with Peter—"then we'll be heroes instead of criminals, right? You can even take credit for sending us there."

Chan leaned back in his chair, hands behind his head. "Okay, one last chance."

"My air tank," Willy said. "It contains pure, concentrated Uranian alien farts, which smells better than anything you've ever smelled in your whole life. You can even take it to a lab for testing."

Chan considered for a moment, then pressed a button on his phone. "Bring in the brat's air tank."

A few minutes later there was a knock at the door. Chan waited for the delivery man to leave, then walked over and hefted the tank in his hands.

"Go ahead. Put on the mouthpiece," Willy said.

Chan eyed him warily.

"Come on," Willy said. "I've been breathing from it all week. No problem."

Chan wrapped his lips around the mouthpiece, turned the valve all the way up, and sucked in a deep breath.

His face went red again, then yellow, then a bright fluorescent green. His eyes spun in their sockets, his hair stood straight up. Then he toppled over like a chopped-down tree and lay motionless on the floor.

"What the–?" Peter said.

"They must've brought in your air tank instead of mine," Willy said.

"So?"

"Well, when you said you were moving to Uranus, I farted into your air tank for revenge. I mean pure, concentrated Grade A fart."

Peter scratched his head. "Hm. No wonder it smelled so bad on that ride back to the spaceship."

Down on the floor, Chan groaned.

"Time to leave this orbit, I think," Willy said. "Three–two–one..."

"Blast off!" they said together, bending over and letting out absolutely, disgustingly green, rancid farts before speeding from the room.

CHAPTER 18

Out of the Clouds

Every seat in the kindergarten activity room was occupied, except for two in the middle of the sixteenth row.

The performance had already started, so people weren't too happy when Willy and Peter squeezed past.

One man scolded: "Sit down. Can't see my daughter. She's playing the haystack."

Peter tore open a bag of garlic-and-Limburger-cheese flavor rippled potato chips, while Willy removed the lid from a container of Moon onion dip. They munched noisily, until someone blurted out: "Can you two kindly keep the noise down? And whatever you're eating stinks like crazy."

Peter belched the Earth's name in Uranian at him.

"Hey, where's Squeaky?" Willy said. "I thought you were carrying his ball."

"I was. I just put him on the floor and... wait a minute...uh oh."

On stage, the kid playing Old MacDonald the farmer tripped over his five-sizes-too-big overalls, while the kids in the chorus, who were all supposed to look like ducks and chickens, sang the song.

The barnyard animals started parading in.

Finally, the chorus got to the line: *"Old MacDonald had some sheep, E-I-E-I-O."*

Two little girls, wearing wool caps and what looked like white bathroom rugs strapped around their bodies, skipped onstage. The second sheep stood on her tippy toes, searching the audience, then stuck out her lip and seemed about to cry.

Willy and Peter rolled their eyes at each other. Then Willy tipped onto his left butt cheek, and Peter tipped onto his right.

A long-drawn-out, sickening, double-whammy fart engulfed the auditorium in thick greenish-gray fumes. People right, left, front, and center gagged and retched.

When the clouds cleared, there were three whole rows of empty seats around Willy and Peter.

Up on stage, Skyler's face lit into a big, sunshiny grin. She waved to the audience and announced:

"Hey, everybody! My big brothers are here!"

FARTY FACTS

for curious minds

Zero-G Gastronauts

Astronauts fart more in space.

That's because in zero gravity, the air in their stomachs can't rise and come out as burps. The burp air mixes with fart gas inside their stomachs, then the digestive muscles push everything all together out the back end.

Which brings up the obvious question on the next page.

Fart Rockets

Do farts act like natural rocket engines in space? The universe needs to know!

When asked whether space explorers actually tried blasting themselves through the air by farting, astronaut Chris Hadfield replied:

"We all tried it. Not the right type of propulsive nozzle."

The fact is, farts do have some propulsive force. In zero gravity and the vacuum of space, you could theoretically fart yourself all the way to the Moon...in 300,000 years.

Space Fart Pollution

NASA scientists worry that farts in space are truly silent-but-deadly.

Besides stinking up spaceships, the methane and hydrogen in astronaut butt gas could actually be a fire hazard.

In 1969 researchers studied how to reduce astronaut farts. They put together two groups of people. One group was fed the same diet as the Gemini space missions. The other ate bland Earth meals. Then they tested their burps and farts.

Not surprisingly, bland food produced less gas. And less fun.

First Fart on the Moon

Astronauts first touched down on the lunar surface in July 1969. But the first confirmed fart on the Moon didn't happen until April 1972.

Apollo 16 astronaut John Young not only farted up a storm while on the Moon, he told the whole universe about it. During a conversation with NASA Mission Control, broadcast live all around the world, Young announced:

"I have the farts again. I got 'em again, Charlie."

Faster than a Flying Fart

Can you out-run a fart?

Farts travel up to 7 miles (11 km) per hour. Most people jog at around 8 miles (13 km) per hour. So that means when you hear a fart, you have a chance to escape?

Not so fast!

At butt level, a fart might be that strong, but it obviously slows down right away as it meets the air around it. So that means you can just walk away, right?

Sorry, no.

Although a fart's wind speed might slow down, the tiny stink molecules quickly spread at 800 feet (243 meters) per second. That's 545 miles (878 km) per hour: nearly the speed of a jet airliner.

Still think you can out-run a fart?

Who writes this stuff?

M.D. WHALEN (writer)

He was always the kid who sat in the back of the class scribbling stories and cartoons. Later he sat in front of the class scribbling stories, when he should have been teaching! Now he writes full time in the back of his house, and has published many books under other names. He also enjoys cycling, world travel, and making rude noises in different languages.

DES CAMPBELL (artist)

Brought up on British comics—Beano, Whizzer & Chips and such—Des has always drawn daft cartoons. He tries to be sophisticated and cultured, but it's all big noses, wonky teeth and funny feet... that's also how his characters look!

Have you read them all?

Can Willy and Peter defeat the evil clowns and save all humanity from ex-*stink*-tion with Weapons of Mass Flatulation?

Did you know that girl farts stink worse than boy farts? Fish farts nearly started a war. How many farts do you inhale on a plane? Learn and laugh with the best-selling encyclopedia of intestinal gas.

Dog farts, cat farts, nurse farts, kids in prison for farting, farting queens and presidents, ancient fart tales. Plus how to fart in other languages. Complete your fart education with volume two!

Is snot good for you? Edible ape boogers, dinosaur snot, snot toothpaste, famous nose pickers in history. Why you should smear snail mucus on your face. Don't be a snot-for-brains; read this book!

Learn more and join the Fart Club at

FARTBOYS.COM